This Boxer book belongs to

. . . .

BOXER BOOKS Ltd. and the distinctive Boxer Books logo
are trademarks of Union Square & Co., LLC.

Union Square & Co., LLC, is a subsidiary of Sterling Publishing Co., Inc.

Text © 2024 Boxer Books
Illustrations © 2024 Sandie Sonke

This edition first published in Great Britain in 2024 by Boxer Books Limited.

ISBN 978-1-915801-66-1

A catalogue record of this book is available from the British Library.

For information about custom editions, special sales, and premium purchases,
please contact specialsales@unionsquareandco.com.

Printed in China
10 9 8 7 6 5 4 3 2 1

01/24

unionsquareandco.com

life's little lessons

Loud Louis

Written by Amber Stewart
Illustrated by Sandie Sonke

BOXER BOOKS

Everywhere that Louis went . . .

a rumbling grey cloud of noise went with him.

"Let's use our indoor voice today, Louis," said his teacher, Miss Jolie, as Louis arrived at nursery.

And Louis did try, because he loved school. He made his voice very small and held the rumbling cloud tight inside him.

But then his favourite green crayon broke and Louis yelled about that.

At breaktime, all the swings were taken, so Louis stomped and hollered about that.

During kickabout, Freya sat on the ball, which went flat as a pancake.

The rumbling cloud inside Louis turned into a thunderstorm and Louis shouted louder and louder.

Across town,
dogs howled.

Cats ran for cover.

Babies on the other side of the world woke up and wailed.

And worst of all, Louis's friends went and sat as far away from Loud Louis and his outside voice as it was possible to be.

And Louis yelled
louder
than ever before.

When Miss Jolie tried to help, he yelled even

louder

so he had to sit by himself for a while.

Then, one day, a new
girl came to nursery.
Her name was Serenity.

Miss Jolie said they should all make
Serenity feel welcome on her first day.

Serenity looked like one big, sunny smile.

Miss Jolie put Serenity with Louis at the art table because they both liked colouring and sticking and making things.

Serenity beamed at him and began colouring
in a tree with a blue crayon. She pressed
so hard that the crayon broke in two.

Louis opened his mouth wide and yelled.
"Please don't yell, Louis," said Serenity.
Her smile wobbled and she put her
hands over her ears.

"Trees are not blue," said Louis, holding back his tears and shouts, "and who can colour with a broken crayon?"

Serenity thought for a moment
and her big smile returned.

She took the broken crayon to Miss Jolie,
who sharpened both pieces.

Serenity kept one half and gave the other half to Louis. "Let's both colour our trees blue."

"Yes, Louis," said Miss Jolie, "your tree can be blue, or pink, or all the colours of the rainbow."

Louis thought about this.

He imagined colouring his rumbling grey mood cloud a sunny yellow – a yellow as sunny as Serenity's smile.

Then they coloured their trees blue.

At breaktime, everyone ran for the swings and there was no space for Louis. So, he whizzed down the slide instead.

Then he took the pancake ball to Miss Jolie and, without shouting, asked her to help.

And Miss Jolie pumped the ball back up fat and round, just right for playing with all his friends.

When school was over for the day, Miss Jolie gave him a special certificate. Louis had never been given a certificate before.

His mum stuck it on the fridge so he could see it every day:

This award goes to Louis
for being kind
and playing nicely.
For using his imagination
and learning that you don't
have to shout to be heard.